Henry - Fisherman

A Story of the Virgin Islands

Marcia Brown

New York   1949

Charles Scribner's Sons

To
Dis, Edward and Barbara
and
the children of St. Thomas

U. S. 883944

Far away in the warm Caribbean sea lies Henry's island. Fish of many colors play in those blue waters, and all day long the winds blow the white sails of the fishing boats in and out of a harbor as safe as heaven itself.

Of course, Henry wanted to be a fisherman, just like his father Jonas. Already Henry could throw a round net over a school of small fish in the shallows. He could spear the big fish that hid in the coral branches in the deeper water. And he could dive and hold his breath under water while he looked for shells.

To be a fisherman, a boy had to be able to dive to anchor the fishpots. He had to dive in the deep water for the conchs, that gave such a rich flavor to a fish stew. And—he had to swim very fast in case a shark was near by.

Henry could hardly wait until he was old enough to go out in the early morning with his father and the other men in the fishing boats. More than anything in the world Henry wanted to go to sea.

"Oh, you'll have to do plenty growing, mon, before you go," his father told him. "You is a good diver, but shark harass you plenty, you so little! He want you for his dinner."

But a boy like Henry could find many things to do on an island like St. Thomas, while he was waiting to grow up and go to sea.

Every morning Henry and his friends brought their tin cans and pails down to the tap by the harbor to get water for the day. Henry loved the walk down the streets of stairs past the gay pink and yellow and green houses, with their little gardens tucked behind the walls. And when you climbed the stairs again with your pail full of water you had to walk straight, straight as the mast on your father's fishing boat, so as not to spill a drop.

Sometimes the children would say, "Let's not go home just yet." Nobody hurried, nobody had to hurry on St. Thomas.

There was always time to strip and dive into the cool water of the harbor. And there was time to look for the wonderful things the tide had left for them along the beach—shells, coral, sea eggs. There was always something different. Once Henry even found an old tire!

When the small fish hurried in toward shore and played around their feet, Henry called out, "Must be shark out in deep water!"

Henry thought about the sea on wash days. While his mother sewed on a new dress for his sister Bianca, he and Bianca did the family washing. While he was hanging the wet clothes on the cactus bushes to dry, they flapped in the wind like the white sails on Jonas' boat, the Ariadne.

Even on market days Henry thought about the sea. Early on Saturday morning he took his wagon to the shady market place in the middle of town. His mother had said, "Henry, you fetch pawpaw, pineapple, bananas and mangoes." When he bit into a mango, the sweet, yellow juice ran down his chin. After he had bought all the fruit his mother needed, he had just five cents left for a bunch of pink frangipanni for the table.

Henry and Bianca had three goats, Jimmy, Annie and Eleanor, that they pastured on a hillside high above the town. When he climbed the hillside to change the tethering pegs of the goats to give them fresh grass, Henry asked Annie for a cup of sweet, rich milk. While he sat resting, the wind chased golden waves up the guinea grass as it chased the waves in to the seashore.

One day Henry's mother said, "How 'bout coconut pudding tonight, Henry?"
So Henry took the long ride on his donkey to the coconut grove. He loved the
grove because it was fresh and cool there and the wind beat on the fronds of
the coconut trees as it beat on a sail at sea.

High up against the sky, in the crowns of the trees, Henry could see the
shiny green and rough brown coconuts. The man in the grove climbed a tall
tree to cut off the nuts. Down they fell with a thud. "Want a drink?" he called,
as he slid down the tree. He lopped off the top of a green coconut with his knife
so that Henry could drink the clear milk inside. "Mm," said Henry, "good!" Then
he scooped out the sweet, white jelly with the piece of the shell.

But most of Henry's time was spent down on the wharf. Here came the boats loaded with charcoal and mangoes from the island of Tortola. Here came the fishing boats with parrot fish, angel fish, grunts and snappers. Here came the boats loaded with pink conchs and green sea turtles, so good for soup.

But best of all, here came the Ariadne, his father's boat. Jonas lowered the mainsail and brought his boat up to the wharf. As he tossed the rope to Henry, he called out, "I need a helper tomorrow, mon. You is young. But you is plenty good diver. How 'bout fishing in the morning?" Henry danced for joy.

That night Henry could hardly get to sleep for thinking about the next morning. He could hear the clacking of the palm branches and the tiny drumming of many insects in the bushes. Underneath all the other sounds was the grind of the pebbles the waves washed up on the harbor beach.

The shutters of the town were still tightly closed against the night when Henry and Jonas went down to the dock. The Ariadne was waiting for them. Jonas pulled the ropes of the mainsail while Henry pushed off. "Come wind, fill the sail!" As they glided away from the dock they could hear the doves in the hills tuning up their morning song. A breeze came and they headed for the open sea.

All morning long they pulled in their lines and dragged in the nets heavy with shining fish. They found the driftwood buoy that showed where the fishpot was anchored. "You dive down, mon, and unhook the pot," Jonas told Henry. So Henry dove down to loosen the pot from the rope that anchored it to a rock, down where the water grew dark. He could see the fishpot full of porgy, hinds, angel fish and groupers. He did not see the long, green shadow gliding along behind him.

But Jonas was watching. Henry shot up to the surface of the water just in time to see a great shark leap almost out of the water after him! Jonas hauled Henry quickly over the side of the boat. "Give thanks, mon! You is sweet meat for sharks!"

At last the boat was filled with fish. "Now we go, mon. What a fisherman you is!" said Jonas proudly.

As the Ariadne sailed into the harbor Henry could see Bianca and his mother in the crowd on the wharf. He put a conch shell to his lips and blew. His mother and Bianca knew it had been a good catch.

As the Ariadne drew near the wharf Henry held up his string of fish. "Plenty good fish today, mon!" the people shouted. "Plenty good fish today!" As Jonas and Henry lifted the boxes of fish out of the boat Jonas said, "Shark almost got Henry today. But Henry is plenty good diver, too fast for old Mister Shark!" Bianca's eyes grew big and round. His mother shook her head. But Henry grinned. It's not every boy that meets a shark on his first fishing trip.

All the way home Henry told Bianca and his mother all about the shark. "Too fast for old Mr. Shark!" he chuckled. "Too fast for old Mister Shark!"

That night as his mother brought in the steaming fungee and a great platter of fried fish, she called to Henry, "Sit down, mon, and partake. You is a fisherman now, for true!"

And after that every morning Henry went out with Jonas on the Ariadne with all the other white sails on the blue sea.